E
FRI   Friskey, Margaret   c. 2
         Seven diving ducks

DATE DUE

APR 08 2008			
DEC 01 2014			

Demco, Inc. 38-293

© THE BAKER & TAYLOR CO.

Seven Diving Ducks

by Margaret Friskey

pictures by Jean Morey

 CHILDRENS PRESS, CHICAGO

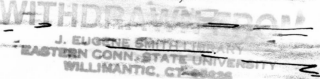

Library of Congress Catalog Card Number: 65-20889

Copyright, 1940, David McKay Company

New Edition
Copyright © 1965, Childrens Press
All rights reserved. Printed in the U.S.A.
Published simultaneously in Canada

6 7 8 9 10 11 12 13 14 15 16 17 18 19 20 21 22 23 24 25   R   75 74 73 72

Once there were six diving ducks.

They lived with their father and mother

in a little house in the apple orchard.

There was also a seventh little duck.
But he wouldn't dive, so they didn't
count him.

One day when the apple trees were
in full bloom, Mother Duck called all
seven fluffy little ducks together.

She took them down to the water's edge
where the white petals of the blossoms
were floating down and settling gently
on the pond.

"My children," said Mother Duck, "it
is time for you to learn to swim."

She looked proudly at her little
family.

"It is not enough for you to scratch
for bugs as the chickens do," she said.
"You must have some fresh fish every day
to make you grow big and strong.

"To catch a fish you must learn to
swim. Follow me!"

Mother Duck walked into the water.

Six little ducks followed her.

"Swimming is just as easy as walking for a duck," she said. "Walk into the

water until you float. Then push with your little webbed feet and you will go. Try it. One, two. One, two."

Six little ducks tried it.
But the seventh little duck did
not like the water.

He stayed close to the shore where
he could keep one foot on the bottom.

That night all the little ducks
were very tired.
    Six of them went to sleep.
    The seventh little duck was tired,
too. But he could not go to sleep.

Father Duck, who had watched the
swimming lesson, made him stay up
and practice swimming on an old
stump.
One, two.
One, two.

"I won't have any sissies in my family,"
said Father Duck sternly. "You might just
as well go and live with the chickens if
you can't learn to swim."

The seventh little duck was very unhappy.
He worked hard. One, two. One, two.

Every day he went into the cold water
with the six other little ducks and he
practiced swimming.

He pushed the water with his webbed feet.
One, two. One, two.

Finally, he learned to swim as well as
the six other ducks. He was very happy!
Then there came a day when all the
blossoms had fallen off the apple trees.
Little green apples had begun to grow.

Again, Mother Duck called all her little
ducks to her.

"Now that you all can swim," she said,
"it is time for you to learn to dive for
fish. Follow me!"

Mother Duck swam all around the pond.
The seven little ducks swam all around
the pond after her. One, two. One, two.

"To catch a fish," said Mother Duck to her children, "you must dive for it like this." And down she went, head first.

When she came up, she had a fish.

Then six little ducks tried it.
They dove again and again until each
had a little fish. After that, the six
little diving ducks had fresh fish every
day.

But the seventh little duck was afraid to put his head in the water, so he had none.

One day when summer was almost gone and the little green apples had grown big and red, Father Duck called his family to him.

"There is no room in a duck family," he said sternly, "for a little duck who will not dive."

The six little diving ducks looked at
the seventh little duck who hung his head.

"The time has come," said Father Duck
to the seventh little duck, "for you to
swim across the pond and live with the
chickens. Go!"

The seventh little duck, who was very
forlorn indeed, set off across the
pond.

Six unhappy little diving ducks, who
were fond of their timid little brother,
lined up on the shore to watch him go.

Sadly he swam across the pond. Just before he reached the other side, where the chickens lived, a big red apple fell on his head — kerplunk.

And down he went in a perfect dive.

"Look what has happened," said Father and Mother Duck and the six little diving ducks.

Very much to his surprise, the seventh little duck caught a fish.

"Why there's nothing to it," he thought as he turned and proudly swam back to show the others the fish he had caught.

"Well done," said Father Duck. "You weren't really afraid to dive at all. You were just afraid to try." Father Duck was proud of his seventh little duck.

The seventh little duck was never
afraid to dive after that.

So the seven little diving ducks and
their father and mother lived happily ever
after in the little house in the apple
orchard.